SCOOBY-DOO!

and the

MONSTER
of MEXICO

JUNIOR NOVELIZATION

SCOOBY-DOO!
and the
MONSTER of MEXICO

JUNIOR NOVELIZATION

Adapted by Jenny Markas from the script by Douglas Wood

SCHOLASTIC INC.

New York   Toronto   London   Auckland   Sydney
Mexico City   New Delhi   Hong Kong   Buenos Aires

ISBN 0-439-44919-7

12 11 10 9 8 7 6 5 4   3 4 5 6 7 8 9/0
Designed by Louise Bova
Special thanks to Duendes del Sur for interior illustrations.
Printed in the U.S.A.
First printing, October 2003

Chapter 1

One soft warm evening in the seaside city of Veracruz, Mexico, a young boy and his father were making
beautiful music together. They were jamming with a
marimba band, hitting the keyboards with little hammers
as they performed for the brightly dressed tourists and locals gathered in the Plaza de Armas. The city's central
square was filled with the scent of blooming flowers and
the glow of thousands of tiny colored lights.

A tiny Chihuahua with big brown eyes lay at the little
boy's feet, happily chewing on a bone as her tail moved in
time to the music.

Suddenly, the dog stopped chewing. Her ears pricked
forward as she sat up to look around. What was it that
only she could hear over the music?

Her eyes came to rest on a hulking dark shadow, over
in the corner of the plaza between a hotel and a closed-up
shop. Bravely — or was she just curious? — the little dog
ran toward the shadow.

"Chiquita!" called the little boy, throwing down his
sticks as he watched his dog disappear between the buildings. The boy ran to follow her.

Seeing his child run off, the father, too, threw down his sticks. "Jorge!" he shouted. "Jorge!" He raced through the plaza, searching desperately for his son.

Meanwhile, the dog trotted along, following the scent of the shadow to the end of the alley and beyond, down a street leading straight to a wharf. The boy ran after her. As he raced toward the wharf, his father turned the corner and spotted him. "Jorgito!" he cried.

Down on the wharf, Chiquita's ears perked up again. This time, the fur rose on the back of her neck. What was that sound? The night air was filled with a loud, low growl, unlike the growl of any dog. Chiquita began to shake.

Just then, someone approached the tiny dog from behind. She shook even harder until she saw who it was. With relief, she scrambled up into Jorge's arms. The boy hugged his dog tightly, and they both stared into the green glow that surrounded them as the hulking shadow drew closer.

Two hands reached out for the boy and his dog. Jorge opened his mouth to scream. Then he realized that it was his own father, Alejo, rescuing him.

Holding his son close, Alejo drew in a breath as he stared at the shadow. "El Chupacabra," he whispered.

He turned and began to run back toward the plaza, still clutching Jorge and Chiquita in his arms.

"El Chupacabra!" he cried, his voice growing louder and louder. "El Chupacabra!"

Screams of terror filled the air. The plaza emptied in a flash as everyone ran for their lives.

Chapter 2

Meanwhile, back in the United States, Fred was checking his e-mail. There was a message from his Mexican pen pal, Alejo Otero.

"I would love for you and your friends to enjoy a relaxing stay with my family here in Veracruz," Alejo wrote. "It'll be great to finally meet my American pen pal."

Fred wrote back right away. "Sounds great! And I can practice my Spanish." Then he wrote to Daphne.

"Jeepers! You've Got Mail!"

Daphne clicked on the mail icon and read Fred's message. She answered his invitation immediately. "Of course I'd like to go to Mexico! Yes! I mean, *¡Sí!* Let's ask Velma!"

"Jinkies! You've Got Mail!"

Velma clicked, got the message, and answered right away. "Mexico? The art! The museums! The pyramids! I'm *there!*"

"Like, You've Got Mail!"

Scooby reached out to click the mail icon with his paw. Shaggy read the message. "Mexico?" he said to

Scooby. "Tomorrow? Like, let me check." He punched some keys on his Palm Pilot. "What've we got tomorrow, Scoob? Let's see ... daydreaming at ten, napping ... snoozing ... relaxing ..." He shook his head. "Looks like we're booked!"

Velma IM'ed just then. "Do you realize we'll be there for the annual Day of the Dead celebration?" she asked.

The name of the holiday alone sent Scooby running under the bed.

"Like, what's that?" asked Shaggy.

"A holiday," Velma told him, "in which families gather at cemeteries to celebrate their ancestors, who are allowed to come back to Earth for two days."

"Cemeteries?" Shaggy asked. "Sounds scary."

From beneath the bed, Scooby nodded.

"Not at all!!" Velma promised. "Just a bunch of kids in costumes, lots of skeleton-shaped cookies, and candy. Basically, it's nonstop eating."

That brought Scooby out from under the bed. Now he was smiling.

So was Shaggy. "Sounds like Halloween!" he said.

"So, what do you say?" Velma asked.

"Can't talk now! Like, Scooby and I gotta pack!"

Signing off, Shaggy ran to the closet for a huge suitcase. "Like, let's start with the essentials," he told Scooby.

Moments later, the suitcase was crammed with donuts, soda, sandwiches, and a big chocolate layer cake. Shaggy looked it over, nodding. "Looks like that's everything," he said.

Scooby shook his head. "Ruh-uh," he said.

"Like, what did I forget?" Shaggy asked.

Scooby dashed into the kitchen and came running back with a big jar.

"Salsa!" said Shaggy, putting it into the suitcase and shutting the lid. Mexico was going to be awesome.

Chapter 3

Early the next morning, the Mystery Machine left the city and rolled down the highway, heading south. The gang watched out of the window as their van zoomed through the little towns on the way to the border. More than one town had a gigantic billboard advertising Mister Smiley's Fantastic Funland, featuring a gigantic picture of Mister Smiley himself.

The tourist attractions in Mexico were a little tamer than Mister Smiley's. Soon after they crossed the border, the gang stopped for a mule ride. Then they had lunch near a bunch of cactuses — and Shaggy sat on one by mistake! After that, they went shopping. Fred got a sombrero, Daphne got some beautiful turquoise jewelry, and Velma got an orange poncho that matched her turtleneck perfectly! Meanwhile, Shaggy and Scooby shopped for goodies, stuffing themselves with tacos, burritos, and tamales.

Finally, the Mystery Machine entered Veracruz and pulled up near a small adobe building.

"Are you sure this is the place?" Shaggy asked, staring at the tiny house.

Fred checked the address Alejo had sent him. "Yeah, this is it," he answered.

"Like, it looks kind of —" Shaggy began.

"Quaint?" asked Daphne.

"Small!" finished Shaggy.

"How are we all going to fit in there?" asked Velma.

"We'll manage somehow," Daphne told her.

Just then, Alejo stepped out of the doorway. *"Hola, mis amigos!"* he said. "Welcome to Mexico!" He reached out to shake Fred's hand. "You must be Fred," he said.

"That's right," said Fred. "And you must be Alejo. Let me introduce you to the gang. This is —"

"No need," Alejo interrupted, smiling. "They're exactly as you described." He shook hands all around. "Please, let me introduce you to my family."

The gang started toward the adobe building, but Alejo turned to walk the other way. He turned back to see why nobody was following him.

"Isn't this where you live?" Fred asked, pointing to the small building.

Alejo cracked up. "No!" he said. "Those are just the guest cottages. You will each have your own." He pointed in the opposite direction. *"This* is where we live."

The gang turned around. They saw a huge hotel, elegant and sprawling, with its main entrance facing the Plaza de Armas.

"Welcome to my family's hotel," Alejo told them. "La Villa Bella."

Chapter 4

Fred's jaw dropped open. "Wow! It's beautiful. What does *'bella'* mean?"

"Beautiful," Alejo translated.

Fred was embarrassed. He should have remembered that. "Oh. Well, La Villa Bella is very *bella*!" he said, blushing.

"Reah," said Scooby. "Rery rella!"

That made Alejo laugh. "Let me show you around," he said, leading the gang into the hotel's courtyard and toward a big beautiful swimming pool. Lounging next to its shimmering blue waters were two women, one younger and one older. "This is my wife, Sofia," Alejo said, "and my mother, Doña Dolores."

"Bienvenidos!" said Doña Dolores.

"Welcome," echoed Sofia, in English.

"And in the pool is the rest of my family," Alejo said, gesturing toward the crowd of splashing, giggling kids who were playing in the water. "Jorge, Oliver, Natalia, Cristina, Fernanda, Carolina, Mirelia, Gabriella, and Sebastian." He ran out of breath as he finished.

"And this is Chiquita!" announced Jorge, patting his tiny dog on the head.

Scooby had been staring at the Chihuahua since the gang had entered the courtyard. He was obviously in love.

"Wow!" said Fred, gazing at the crowd of kids. "Are they all your children?"

Alejo and Sofia started to laugh. "No, no, no!" said Alejo, waving his hands. "Only Jorgito. The rest are just visiting for the Day of the Dead festivities. Here in Mexico, family is *muy importante*."

Sofia spoke up. "You must be hot and tired after your long trip," she said to the gang. "Please feel free to join the children in the pool."

Scooby didn't hesitate for a second. Glancing at Chiquita, he climbed all the way up to the very top of the high dive. Below him, the children moved to the sides of the pool, waiting to see what would happen. Scooby took a deep breath and did a beautiful swan dive — ending in a massive belly flop that sent water flying everywhere. The kids shrieked and laughed as Scooby surfaced right under Chiquita. He looked up at her adoringly as she, perched on his head, giggled and fluttered her eyelashes down at him.

Sofia smiled. "I think Scooby has already won somebody's heart," she said. "Now, how about a visit to the café?" She pointed the way to the hotel's indoor/outdoor café, which was run by Luis, Alejo's brother. He looked a little like Alejo, except for his gloomy expression. His fiancée, Charlene, was blond and spoke with a strong Texas twang. The two of them managed the café together.

"Howdy!" said Charlene, when Alejo introduced the gang. "Lemme grab y'all a cup of caffay lay-chair-a while you take a load off." She ran to get their coffees, leaving them with a glum-looking Luis.

"You can see why I fell head over heels for her," he said, watching Charlene walk away. "I met her on my last trip to the United States, at Mister Smiley's Fantastic Funland. I've been smiling ever since."

The gang nodded, looking a little puzzled. Luis sure had a different idea of what "smiling" meant.

Charlene came back with a tray of empty glasses and a big kettle. She poured thick black coffee into each glass. "*Cafe lechera* is famous in Veracruz," Luis explained. "First one server pours you thick coffee, then the custom is to bang on your glass with a spoon" — he did this as he talked — "until another server arrives to pour hot milk into your glass." He grabbed an aluminum pitcher full of hot milk and began to pour.

"Isn't that a hoot?" Charlene asked. "I just love these *'loco'* customs. That's 'crazy' in Mexican." She giggled and corrected herself. "I mean, Spanish."

Scooby was staring at Shaggy's coffee, licking his lips and drooling a little. Shaggy noticed. "Like, Scooby, don't be rude!" he said.

"Looks like we forgot someone," said Alejo.

Charlene poured some milk and coffee into a big bowl and set it down for Scooby. He lapped it right up while she was still bent over. A few coffee grounds fell out of Charlene's pockets as she straightened up. "Ya know," she said, brushing the brown specks away, "some days I grind so many coffee beans, I swear the little suckers are comin' outta my ears!"

At that, Scooby looked up, showing off a big milk mustache.

Velma laughed. "It didn't take Scooby long to start 'livin' the *vida* mocha!'"

Chapter 5

A little later, the gang and their new *amigos* sat down to lunch. In Veracruz, even lunch was an occasion for a *fiesta,* Doña Dolores explained as she passed around platters heaped with delicious spicy food.

"This *carne asada* is wonderful, Doña Dolores," said Daphne.

"Yeah," Shaggy agreed. "Like, whoever came up with the whole *fiesta* tradition is okay in my book."

Alejo nodded, smiling. "It is often followed by another tradition," he told Shaggy. "La *siesta,* afternoon nap."

"Even better!" said Shaggy, happily.

"Reah, reven retter!" echoed Scooby.

Velma spoke up. "The purpose of *fiestas* and *siestas,* Shaggy," she informed her friend, "is to provide sustenance and rest for *another* tradition: hard work."

Shaggy looked alarmed. "Traditions," he said quickly. "Like, who needs 'em?"

Scooby made a face. "Rucch!"

Everyone at the table cracked up. But their laughter was cut short by the sudden appearance of a tall man dressed all in black. He stepped up to the table, looking very serious. "Forgive me for interrupting your meal,

Doña Dolores," he said politely, "but I need to discuss some business matters with your sons."

Doña Dolores answered in the same polite tone. "As you wish, Señor Fuente."

Alejo and Luis stood up. So did Charlene, linking arms with Luis. She wasn't about to be left out. "Excuse us, please," Alejo said. "This won't take long."

The three of them and Señor Fuente headed for the far corner of the courtyard and began to talk, gesturing and pointing almost as if they were arguing. Nobody at the table could quite hear what they were saying.

Doña Dolores saw that the gang looked bewildered. Leaning forward, she whispered, "Diego Fuente used to do business with my late husband. I don't trust him, never did. He is a — how do you say in America?"

"Crook?" Fred asked.

"Liar?" Daphne suggested.

"Con man?" Velma added.

Doña Dolores suddenly found the word she was looking for. "Jerk!" she said.

Just then, the foursome in the corner began to argue more loudly so that the gang could hear what they were saying. "For the last time," Alejo was telling Señor Fuente, "I told you, no! Now, please leave. We have guests."

Señor Fuente turned toward the table. "I apologize for the disturbance," he said, with a little bow. "Please, finish your meal." He stalked off, and Alejo, Luis, and Charlene came back to the table.

Alejo rolled his eyes. "That man is as stubborn as a bull," he said. "He wants to buy our father's land and he won't take no for an answer."

Luis shrugged. "Maybe it is not such a bad idea," he said hesitantly. "Putting all your assets into land is foolish."

Alejo turned to him, his eyes flashing. "We made a promise to Papa before he died," he said. "I don't intend to break it now."

Sofia cleared her throat. It was time to change the subject. "So," she said to the gang, "how will you be spending your first full day in Veracruz?"

"We were hoping to watch the preparations for the Day of the Dead festivities," Velma told her.

Doña Dolores frowned. "If anyone's still alive to honor the dead," she said in a low voice.

Shaggy heard her loud and clear. "What?" he asked nervously.

"Rhat?" Scooby's ears were perked up.

Charlene looked around at the gang. "Don't y'all know about the big ol' monster?"

Chapter 6

At that moment, as if on cue, the sky darkened. Thunder boomed, rattling the dishes on the table, and a streak of lightning shot across the sky. It started to pour, soaking everyone to the skin within seconds. They all leaped up and ran inside.

While Doña Dolores, Sofia, Charlene, and Jorge went off to get dry, Luis and Alejo and the gang gathered around the gigantic fireplace in the hotel's main lodge.

It was time for some explanations.

Alejo took a deep breath. "You must have noticed by now that the hotel is relatively empty," he said to the gang. "That's because a monster has been terrorizing Veracruz and the nearby villages. Right after I sent that e-mail to you, the monster showed up near the plaza and nearly got Jorgito."

Shaggy and Scooby gulped and exchanged wide-eyed looks.

Alejo looked down at his hands. "I immediately e-mailed you again, to warn you, but you must have already left."

Shaggy was still looking scared. "Did you say m-m-monster?" he asked.

Alejo nodded. "Yes," he answered. "The locals call him El Chupacabra."

Velma gasped. "I've read about him!" she said. "He's Mexico's version of Bigfoot."

Scooby's mouth fell open. "Rigfoot?" he asked.

"That's right," Luis said.

Alejo held up a hand. "I am not a superstitious man," he told them, "but I saw it with my own eyes, down by the wharf. I will never forget it. He stands nearly ten feet tall and walks on two hind legs. He's covered with thick fur and has the face of a hideous monkey, with huge paws and sharp fangs."

Shaggy and Scooby were hugging each other and shaking. But there was even more.

"He moves with the speed of a jaguar," Alejo continued, "and his eyes glow green like those of a demon."

That did it. Scooby jumped up and started running. He tripped over a coffee table and fell. His tail went into the fire. Scooby jumped up again, screaming. That scared Shaggy, and he started screaming, too. That scared all the others, and soon the whole room was full of shrieking.

Fred leaped to his feet. "Calm down, everybody!" he shouted. "El Chupacabra's only a *myth*!"

The screaming stopped. Alejo reached out to pat Scooby's head. "Yes," he said, "let's forget about El Chupacabra and make the most of your first visit to Mexico."

Sofia and Charlene came in just then. "Why don't we all get a good night's sleep?" Sofia asked, trying to calm everyone down.

"Yes," Alejo agreed. "There's nothing to worry about."

"Alejo's right," Daphne said, as if convincing herself.

"But just in case," Luis warned, "double lock your doors . . ."

"Say your prayers . . ." Charlene added.

"And whatever you do . . ." Luis began.

Charlene joined him in a final warning. "DON'T GO OUTSIDE!"

Chapter 7

Locked into their cottage, Shaggy and Scooby were trying to get to sleep. Shaggy spoke up. "Like, whoever heard such a ridiculous story?" he asked. "A ten-foot-high hairy monster with big feet and sharp teeth? Sounds like something out of a silly cartoon!"

Shaggy sounded brave. But it was just big talk. He and Scooby were huddled in their beds, gripping the fireplace tools in case they needed weapons. Both of them wore whistles around their necks, and their eyes were wide-open. Every bit of furniture in the cottage was stacked against the front door, and there was a bucket of water rigged up over the door, ready to drop on an intruder.

"Well, pleasant dreams, Scoob," Shaggy said. "See you in the morning."

Scooby nodded, but he looked nervous.

Shaggy's eyes were still wide-open. "Like, it's going to be a long night," he sighed.

Just then, they heard a loud rustling noise from outside. Shaggy sat up in bed. "Did you hear that? Sounds like something outside the window." He clutched his pillow.

Scooby nodded.

"Probably just a little Mexican bird or a squirrel," Shaggy said. There was a moment of silence, then some more rustling. That was all it took. Shaggy jumped out of bed and started running around in circles, blowing his whistle. "El Caba-choo-choo!" he yelled. "I mean, La Kooka-babka! Like, El Popa-Chooopa! No, I mean — HELP!"

Scooby started running around in circles, too, blowing his own whistle. The room was total chaos. Scooby ran over to the window.

"No, Scoob! He's trying to break in!" Shaggy shouted, running toward the door. He and Scooby both tripped over the wires leading to their nightstand lamps. *Bang! Crash!* They went down hard, and so did the lamps, plunging the room into total darkness.

Shaggy screamed. So did Scooby. They both blew their whistles.

"Like, we're trapped!" yelled Shaggy. "Let's get out of here!"

A few minutes later, Shaggy's soot-covered head popped out through the cottage's chimney. Behind him, Scooby popped out, shaking ash out of his ears. They looked down to the ground and saw Fred and Velma far below.

"What happened to you two?" Fred asked. He was dressed in pajamas with a matching scarf.

"And what was all that noise?' Velma asked. Her hair was in curlers.

Shaggy and Scooby crawled down from the roof and jumped the last few feet. "Like, that big Mexican Bigfoot was trying to get us!" Shaggy reported.

"Oh, no!" Fred said. "Where's Daphne?"

They all ran over to the next cottage. Fred was about to knock on her door when all four of them saw it at the same time: a pair of glowing green lights!

Shaggy and Scooby stopped in their tracks and did a quick about-face, but Fred and Velma grabbed them. "Oh, no you don't," Velma said. "This is no time to be chicken. It's all for one and one for all!"

Shaggy grimaced. "Like, I've always felt that teamwork was highly overrated," he said.

"Reah," Scooby said, nodding.

"Okay, guys," Fred said, ignoring them both. "On the count of three, we'll charge the door. Ready? ONE! TWO! THREE!"

"CHARGE!" they all said at once, running toward the door.

At that moment, Daphne opened her door. The rest of the gang came barreling through, winding up in a big pile at the far side of the room — right next to Daphne's nightstand, which held a CD player with two glowing green lights.

Fred picked it up and examined the "Power" and "Play" buttons. "We thought these were the eyes of El Chupacabra," he said, embarrassed.

Daphne pulled off her headphones. "Sorry, guys," she said. "I was afraid to go to sleep and thought some Latin rhythms would calm me down. Looks like everyone was riled by Alejo's stories."

Just then, Shaggy's head popped out of the heap. "Like, anybody got a bandage?" he asked.

The gang got themselves untangled and headed outside. "I don't know what you heard, guys," Fred said, shining his flashlight near Shaggy and Scooby's cottage, "but I think we're all safe now. Let's all try to get some — wait a minute! What's this?" He pointed his light at the ground below Shaggy's window.

"Footprints!" Daphne gasped. "Big ones."

Shaggy and Scooby didn't even want to see. They both covered their eyes. "Don't look, Scoob," Shaggy told his pal, "or we'll never get to sleep!"

Velma waved her flashlight along the trail of footprints. "Notice how they lead to the cottage window, then reverse direction and head off toward the hotel?"

Fred nodded. "Whatever it was, was brave enough when we were separated, but got scared at the thought of a bunch of us to contend with. Not a very courageous monster."

Velma started toward her cottage, yawning. "Well, whatever it is, it's gone. Maybe now we can all get some sleep."

"We're gonna need it," agreed Fred. "We've got a big day tomorrow."

Shaggy nodded. "Yeah! Sightseeing and chocolate tamales! Can't wait!"

Scooby licked his lips.

"That's not exactly what I meant, Shaggy," Fred said.

Shaggy and Scooby looked at him, confused.

"We've got a mystery on our hands," Fred explained.

"Zoinks!" said Shaggy.

Chapter 8

The next morning, Alejo and Luis helped the gang pack up the Mystery Machine for a day of sightseeing. Scooby and Chiquita said good morning to each other as Fred and Velma filled the brothers in on what had happened the night before.

Daphne joined them. She opened up the bag she was carrying and pulled something out. "I got up early," she explained, "and used my mud face mask to make a cast of Bigfoot's big foot." She showed them the cast.

"Wow," Alejo said. "It is huge!"

"And look," Luis pointed out. "It is speckled with some kind of gritty black stuff."

Fred leaned forward. "Is it dirt?" he asked.

"I don't think so," Velma said, also taking a closer look. "I don't know *what* it is."

"Well, whatever it is," Alejo said, waving at the cast, "please do not mention it to my mother or Sofia."

Luis nodded. "Or Charlene. I don't want to scare them."

"In fact," Alejo added, "I better alert the security guards to be especially vigilant."

"If word of this gets out," Luis said, "we will lose the few tourists we have managed to keep. El Chupacabra could ruin our livelihood, not to mention everyone else's in Veracruz." He looked more glum than ever.

"Don't worry," Fred assured them both. "No matter how huge, ferocious, or bloodthirsty this vicious Chupacabra monster may be —"

Daphne held out the cast of the humongous footprint and finished Fred's thought. "We'll get to the bottom of this mystery. You can count on us. Right, gang?"

Velma and Fred were nodding in agreement as Shaggy and Scooby poked their heads out of the van and got their first look at the footprint.

Scooby reached out a paw to compare sizes. He passed out cold when he saw how much bigger the monster's paw was. He only came to after Chiquita waved her tiny Spanish fan over his nose.

When the van was all packed, the gang climbed inside along with Luis and Alejo. Sofia, Doña Dolores, Jorge, Charlene, and Chiquita gathered to wave good-bye. Just as they were about to take off, Charlene ran up to the van. "Oops," she said. "I almost forgot."

Luis rolled down his window, and Charlene handed him a golden medallion. "I know this is silly, hon, but it's a good-luck charm. With that big ol' Bigfoot thang out there, y'all can't be too careful." She hung the charm around Luis's neck. "Promise me you won't *ever* take it off."

Luis nodded. "I promise, Charlene."

Meanwhile, Fred was paging through his Spanish–English dictionary. Before he started up the van, he leaned out the window to speak to Doña Dolores, Sofia, and Charlene. "Um," he began, *"muchas gracias para su hospital generoso y muy deliciosas cometas."*

The women smiled at him, looking a little confused. Fred smiled back, fired up the van, and drove off down the road. Alejo started to laugh.

"What's so funny?" Fred asked him.

Alejo chuckled. "You just thanked my family for their 'generous hospital and delicious comets.'"

Chapter 9

The streets of Veracruz were not exactly bustling. Some locals were out and about, preparing for the Day of the Dead festivities, but there were hardly any tourists. Alejo told the gang that the city was usually much busier, but that the "El Chupacabra incident" had put a real dent in the tourist population.

Velma took out her camcorder, planning to shoot a few scenes to remember the city by.

"I've got an idea," said Fred. "Let's ask the locals about the monster."

"Good idea, Fred," Velma said. "We can videotape them."

Daphne jumped right on that idea. "Great! I can be the reporter." She ran a brush through her hair and jumped out of the Mystery Machine, heading for a group of kids hanging out in a school playground, carving jack-o'-lanterns. Jorge and his cousins were there, and Daphne smiled at them. Then she became Reporter Daphne. She faced the camera Fred held and began to speak. "A see-saw. A jungle gym. A merry-go-round. At first glance this playground looks like any other. But the children here in Veracruz are fearful, and have good reason to be. El

Chupacabra. Imaginary Bigfoot? Or — Big Scary Monster That Could Bite Your Head Off? You decide." She walked over to Jorge and started to interview him and his friends. "What does El Chupacabra look like?" she asked.

"A gorilla!" cried Jorge.

"A bear!" shouted Carolina.

"An alien!" yelled Sebastian.

Daphne nodded wisely. Then she headed for the school kitchen, where some women were baking skeleton cookies. The kitchen smelled spicy and delicious! The videotape showed Scooby and Shaggy in the background, gulping down all the cookies they could grab. The women didn't seem to mind at all.

"Where does El Chupacabra live?" Daphne asked them.

"In the mountains!" said the first one.

The next one disagreed. "In the desert!"

The third one didn't seem to care. She just shrugged.

Daphne moved on, to a wall where a bunch of people were painting a Day of the Dead mural featuring dancing skeletons and a skeleton marimba band. Shaggy joined in, painting a skeleton Shaggy self-portrait. Daphne went into interview mode again. "What does El Chupacabra do?" she asked.

"Eats goats!" said one man.

Another man nodded. "Destroys crops," he added.

"He's a bully," piped up a little girl.

Out on the street, a crowd watched and listened as a band rehearsed. Scooby and Alejo were singing along as Daphne approached. "What does El Chupacabra sound like?" she asked.

"Like a coyote!" said a trumpet player.

"Like an ape!" put in an old woman standing nearby.

The drummer grinned. "Like my Uncle Flaco!"

"And what does he smell like?" Daphne asked.

"Like sulphur," said the trumpet player.

Another woman wrinkled her nose. "Like garbage!"

This time, the drummer cracked up. "Like my Uncle Flaco!"

Daphne nodded seriously and headed off down the street, still talking to the camera. "Is Mexico's Bigfoot some, none, or all of these things?" she mused. "Will he show up tomorrow at the Day of the Dead festivities, or remain as elusive as the Loch Ness Monster or the perfect boyfriend? This is Daphne Blake in Veracruz, reporting. Back to you, Velma."

"And — cut!" shouted Fred.

"Back to *you*?" Velma asked, shaking her head.

Daphne just giggled.

Chapter 10

"**Y**ikes!" said Shaggy, looking at the bright red words scrawled in paint across the psychedelic flowers on the side of the Mystery Machine. The gang had come back to their van to find it vandalized. "What does that mean in English?"

Alejo read the Spanish words aloud. *"Sal ahora! O no verás el día de manana!"*

Fred translated. "'Leave today! Or you won't see tomorrow!' Is that right, Alejo?"

Alejo frowned. "Unfortunately, your translation is correct."

Shaggy shook his head. "Looks like someone wants us to make like a piñata and beat it," he said.

Daphne nodded. "We better get out of here *now*," she said.

In a flash, Scooby and Shaggy had jumped into the van. They buckled their seat belts and sat there, ready to take off.

"Hold on, you two," said Velma. "We came here today to get to the bottom of this Chupacabra mystery —"

"And nobody's going to scare us away until we do!" Fred finished.

Scooby and the gang are on vacation south of the border in Veracruz, Mexico!

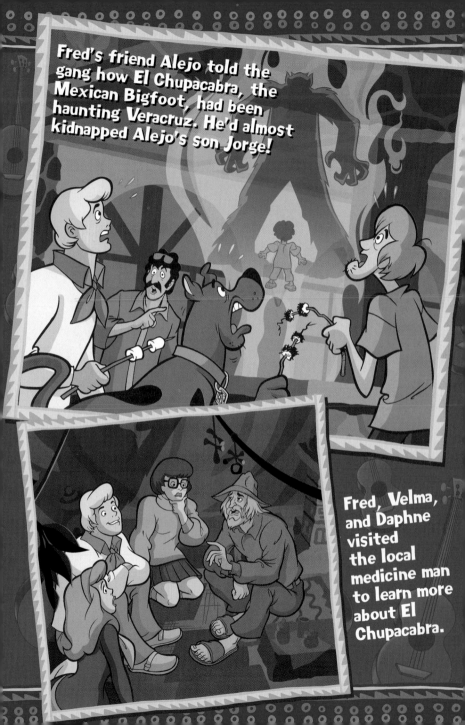

Fred's friend Alejo told the gang how El Chupacabra, the Mexican Bigfoot, had been haunting Veracruz. He'd almost kidnapped Alejo's son Jorge!

Fred, Velma, and Daphne visited the local medicine man to learn more about El Chupacabra.

As soon as they left the shaman's tent, El Chupacabra appeared! The kids ran away as fast as they could.

The next day, the gang visited a museum of Aztec history. A cheerful tour guide showed them around.

At the museum, the gang watched an informational movie. But soon the animals from the movie came alive ...

... and chased after the gang!

The gang escaped. But that night, at a celebration for the Day of the Dead, **El Chupacabra** emerged again!

El Chupacabra got all tied up when it chased Scooby and Shaggy through a string of lights. It was the museum guide!

That night, the gang celebrated the closing of another case. "Rooby-Dooby-Doo!" cheered Scooby.

Shaggy rolled down the window. "Like, it's too late for that," he said.

Velma knew what to do. "Looks like they need some friendly persuasion," she said to Daphne. She pulled a box of Scooby Snacks out of her bag. "Would you each do it for a Scooby Snack?" she asked.

Inside the Mystery Machine, Shaggy and Scooby looked at each other.

Daphne reached into the box and took out two Scooby Snacks. "How 'bout two Scooby Snacks?" she asked.

Shaggy and Scooby looked at each other again. This time, they both nodded. They hopped out of the van and opened wide while Daphne and Velma tossed them their snacks. They crunched happily while Velma started to plan.

"Okay!" she said. "So far, it seems as if El Chupacabra only comes out at night. Now that it's getting dark, we should do a thorough search of the town."

Daphne agreed. "Maybe we'll find a clue to help us find the monster, or at least the 'van vandals.'"

"The girls are right," said Fred. "Alejo and Luis, why don't you investigate the hills?" He gestured to the rolling hills surrounding the city. "The girls and I will search the west part of town, and Shaggy and Scooby can search the east."

Everyone took off in opposite directions, leaving Shaggy and Scooby standing near the Mystery Machine as dusk fell and the sky grew dark. "You know, Scoob," Shaggy said thoughtfully, "the Mystery Machine is actually parked in the east side of town. Why don't we do a thorough search of the van, and if everything checks out okay, just keep guard right here?"

Scooby liked that idea. "Ro-kay!" he said.

The two of them climbed back inside the van. Within seconds, the lights went out. A moment later, the snoring began.

And a moment after *that* . . .

A black-gloved hand, holding a tool, reached under the van. It made a quick motion, pulled back, and disappeared. Then a pool of oily fluid began to ooze out of the van, making a dark puddle on the ground.

Chapter 11

Fred, Velma, and Daphne stumbled along in the dark, finding their way through the outskirts of the west side of Veracruz. Everything was peaceful. Until, that is, the three of them turned a corner and came face-to-face with a huge serpent! The snake was at least as big as Fred.

"Yikes!" they all screamed.

The serpent didn't move.

"It's just a statue," Fred said.

Daphne and Velma sighed with relief. "Yes," said Velma, taking a closer look. "It's Quetzalcoatl, the Feathered Serpent. I've read about him. He was revered by the Aztecs as the god of all things good."

But Daphne and Fred weren't paying attention. Instead, they were staring at a nearby tent — and at the old man coming out of it. "Look!" Daphne said.

When Velma turned, she saw an old Indian man wearing a long-eared cap decorated with shells and feathered snakes. *"Bienvenidos,"* he said. "Welcome."

"Oh, good," Daphne said. "You speak English."

"Yes, of course," said the man, drawing aside the flap of his tent. "Please, come in."

As Fred, Velma, and Daphne ducked to enter the tent, someone was watching from outside. A huge, hairy hand moved aside some shrubbery to get a better look as the threesome joined the old Indian.

The tent was spooky inside, decorated with the skulls of animals, crystals and gems, feathers, and odd-shaped rocks.

"Wow," said Velma, looking around. "Are you a medicine man?"

The Indian sat down and Fred, Velma, and Daphne joined him. "I prefer *curandero,*" he said, "but yes, medicine man, shaman, or healer would all be right, too. How can I help you?"

"We're hoping you can tell us something about El Chupacabra," Velma said, leaning forward.

The *curandero* nodded. "Well," he said, "like everyone, I have heard the stories about the Bigfooted beast. But there is nothing in our ancient lore about a monster such as this. Our animal friends don't harm people for no reason."

Fred looked confused. "Then how do you explain the attacks?"

The *curandero* turned his wise eyes Fred's way. "The only evil force in this land is greed," he said.

"Greed?" Velma asked.

The *curandero* looked sad. "Powerful men from other lands came here to exploit the native people and wipe out our culture. It began with Cortés and the conquistadors hundreds of years ago, but it continues today."

Velma still didn't understand. "But what does this have to do with El Chupacabra?"

"Recently," answered the *curandero,* "people from the north offered huge sums of money to build businesses here and to attract tourists. The locals turned down the offers, but when the strangers left, they vowed to return."

"Hmm," Fred said. "I see."

"You *do*?" asked Daphne.

The *curandero* spoke again. "The answers to all your questions can be found in the past," he said meaningfully. "Oh," he added, "and did I also mention that you're in grave danger?"

Daphne gulped. "Uh, no, I think you skipped that part."

At that, the *curandero* leaned toward the three friends and spoke very solemnly. "You're in grave danger," he said, just as an eerie howling started up outside the tent.

Velma shivered. "We better get back to the others and warn them."

The *curandero* nodded and held up a hand. "Be careful, my friends. In Mexico, things are not always what they seem."

Daphne, Fred, and Velma stood up to leave. As they came out of the tent together, the *curandero* handed them a business card. "If you have any questions, check out my web site at www.AncientWisdom.com," he told them.

"Web site?" Daphne asked, looking at the card in amazement.

"As I said," the old man answered with the hint of a smile, "expect the unexpected."

Fred stepped forward. *"Muchas gracias para sus palabras sabias de avestruz,"* he said to the *curandero.*

The man gave Fred an odd look as the trio walked away.

"What did you say?" Daphne whispered to Fred.

"I thanked him for his wise words of advice," Fred told her.

Meanwhile, the *curandero* watched them leave. "Thanks for your wise words of *ostrich*?" he muttered. "Teenagers. Go figure."

Chapter 12

Meanwhile, over on the east side of Veracruz, Luis and Alejo made their way up into the hills. Their flashlights barely lit up the thick forest as they moved along a nearly invisible path.

Luis stopped suddenly. *"Escucha!"* he said. "Listen!"

There was a fluttering in the trees above them. Alejo shone his flashlight up, just in time to see an owl landing on a branch. "Just an owl," he told his brother. "Don't be a baby."

They kept walking, deeper and deeper into the forest. Luis lagged behind a little, and before long they were far enough apart that they could not see each other. Luis got scared again. "Alejo!" he called. "Let's head back! We're getting nowhere."

"Okay!" Alejo shouted back. Just then, he heard a low growl. He whipped his head around to see something moving beyond a thicket of trees. A green glow fell upon the branches. Then there was another growl. "Luis!" Alejo yelled. "Come quick!"

There was no answer.

"Luis!" Alejo shouted. "Luis!"

The forest was silent.

Suddenly, El Chupacabra burst out of the thicket and leaped toward Alejo! Screaming, Alejo dodged the monster, only to fall backward over a cliff. Reaching out blindly, he managed to grab a root growing from the side of the mountain. Looking down at the ground far, far below him, Alejo did his best to stay calm. With a huge effort, he hauled himself up and began to climb toward the top of the mountain. From above, he could still hear the growling of El Chupacabra.

Back at the Mystery Machine, Shaggy stopped snoring and sat straight up in his seat. "Do you hear what I hear, Scoob?" he asked.

Scooby nodded. He put his hands over his ears to try to shut out El Chupacabra's growling.

"Like, that's not going to help much," Shaggy told his pal. "We better get outta here now, or we're gonna be Chupacabra enchiladas!"

Shaggy jumped behind the wheel of the van, started it up, and took off into the dark night.

Chapter 13

On the west side, Fred, Daphne, and Velma walked down an old dirt road. Daphne turned to Fred. "None of this looks familiar. Are you sure we're going the right way?"

Velma pointed up at the stars sprinkling the sky above them. "That's Polaris," she said, pointing to a particularly bright star. "We should be headed in the opposite direction."

"Trust me," Fred said. "I know where I'm going."

"We're sunk," Daphne whispered to Velma.

On the east side, Alejo was just clambering to the top of the cliff. Luis appeared just in time to give his brother a hand. "Alejo!" Luis said. "What happened?"

"I was attacked by El Chupacabra," Alejo said. "Didn't you hear me calling for help?"

"No," said Luis. "Something hit me over the head and knocked me out. When I woke up, you were gone." He didn't look at his brother as he said this.

"Well," Alejo said, "El Chupacabra is still out there. We've got to find the others before *he* does."

In the Mystery Machine, Shaggy hunched over the wheel as he and Scooby hurtled along, looking for any sign of their friends. "Like, the next time we go on a trip," Shaggy said to Scooby, "remind me to pick somewhere a little less exciting . . . like maybe a librarians' convention?"

Just then, the road tilted downhill toward an intersection with a stop sign.

Shaggy hit the brakes.

The van didn't even slow down.

"Zoinks!" Shaggy shouted. "The brakes aren't working!" He stomped on the brakes again and again, but nothing happened.

Scooby put his paws over his eyes.

The van zoomed right through the intersection, just missing a truck coming in from the left. "Yikes!" yelled Shaggy.

"Rikes!" echoed Scooby.

The van kept on speeding along, right into town. It went faster every time it went downhill, and Shaggy had his hands full swerving to avoid people, dogs, and other cars. "Like, how do you stop this thing?" he yelled.

Scooby peeked through his fingers. The Mystery Machine was headed straight for the ocean.

"Yaaahhhhh!" cried Shaggy and Scooby. They both covered their eyes as the Mystery Machine rolled right onto a pier and sailed off the edge.

The van landed on a ferry that was just pulling up to a dock. When the ferry docked, the Mystery Machine just kept on going, right back up the dock and off again into the streets of Veracruz.

Shaggy and Scooby didn't even notice the ferryman shaking his fist at them.

Chapter 14

"**O**kay, Fred," said Daphne, poking her head through a bush. "How do you say 'hopelessly lost' in Spanish?"

The three friends were deep in the forest, with no idea which way was out.

"It looks like the woods get thicker up ahead," Velma said.

"Do you suppose we'll meet any wild animals?" asked Daphne.

"We might," admitted Fred.

"Mostly coyotes and jaguars and boars," Velma guessed.

Daphne looked scared. "Coyotes?"

"And jaguars?" Fred added.

"And boars," said Velma.

"Oh, my." Daphne shuddered.

As if on cue, the three friends heard a high-pitched yipping coming from some trees nearby. The sound got louder and louder, as if the animal were coming closer.

"Let's get out of here!" yelled Fred, taking off at a fast run. The others followed him without looking. *Wham!* All three of them ran right into Luis and Alejo.

"Oof!" said Fred, rubbing his head. "Sorry, guys."

"No, *we're* sorry," Alejo answered. "We were hoping to find you close by, but not *that* close."

Daphne held up a hand. "We thought we heard El Chupacabra. Listen."

The yipping started up again.

"That is nothing to be afraid of," said Luis. "It is just a coyote."

"There are lots of them around here," added Alejo. "They are more afraid of you then you are of them."

"Then why is it headed in our direction?" Fred asked.

Luis thought for a moment. "Maybe it is not running toward us, but *away* from something else."

"Yeah, " said Daphne. "But what?"

Just then, a coyote burst into the clearing. It hardly seemed to notice the five humans standing there as it galloped right by and raced off into the distance.

Then the friends heard a long, low growl.

"Like, maybe *that!*" Velma said, answering Daphne's question with a wave at the nearby trees.

There, peeking through the branches, was a huge hairy beast. It was about ten feet tall, with dark brown fur and gigantic feet. Its glowing green eyes seemed to pierce the night as it stared straight back at them. It opened its mouth, showing huge sharp teeth, and let out the loudest growl yet.

"Jinkies!" yelled Velma. "El Chupacabra!"

"Run!" shouted Alejo.

They all took off, with the monster chasing them. They didn't stop running until they reached the streets of Veracruz. They headed straight for the spot where they'd left the Mystery Machine.

"I think we lost it," panted Alejo, looking behind them for El Chupacabra.

But Daphne was looking at the empty parking spot. "Oh, no! The Mystery Machine!"

"It's gone!" said Fred. He couldn't believe it.

Velma pointed to an oily spot on the ground. "But its brake fluid isn't," she said seriously. "Someone must have tampered with the brakes on the Mystery Machine."

They all stared down at the spot. Then they heard something. Another loud growl.

"No time to find out who or why," said Luis.

"We've got to find Shaggy and Scooby!" Fred said.

Velma cupped her hands around her mouth and yelled. "Shaggy!"

Daphne did the same. "Scooby-Doo! Where are you?"

Chapter 15

"**R**ooooaaarrr!" El Chupacabra jumped out of the shadows. Everybody scattered.

The monster watched them run. Then he picked the closest target: Fred. Roaring, he lumbered after him, though the dark, empty streets. Fred looked over his shoulder and saw the monster gaining on him. Then he looked ahead and saw a ladder leaning against an adobe building. He scrambled up it as fast as he could.

El Chupacabra followed him.

Fortunately, the weight of the monster was too much for the ladder. The rungs broke away as he stepped on them, leaving Fred standing on a tall pair of stilts. He ran off, leaving El Chupacabra empty-handed.

Next, the monster spotted Daphne running down the street. He took off after her.

Daphne didn't even take time to scream. When she spotted a chicken coop in front of her, she ran right into it.

El Chupacabra followed her.

A moment later, El Chupacabra stuck his head up through the roof of the coop. Broken eggs ran down his hairy face, and a chicken pecked him on the top of his head. The monster shook his head, and feathers flew all over. He looked around and saw Velma slipping around a corner.

Velma saw the monster coming after her and ran straight for a prickly, spiny cactus garden in front of a small hotel.

El Chupacabra followed her.

Velma whipped off her orange wool poncho, revealing the matching turtleneck beneath it. She placed the poncho over a big cactus, just about her size and shape. She took off her glasses and stuck them on the cactus's "face." Then she ducked behind the cactus and waited.

"Owww!" El Chupacabra howled as he grabbed the Velma cactus. Velma's glasses flew through the air and landed right on her face. The monster leaped in pain and bounced into another cactus, then another. When he finally managed to free himself, he looked around and spotted Luis and Alejo racing down the street.

Growling and picking thorns out of his fur, El Chupacabra followed them.

Luis and Alejo ran toward a movie theater, where they spotted Fred, Daphne, and Velma. All five of them tugged at the doors, only to find out that the theater was locked up tight. El Chupacabra was getting closer and closer.

The friends squeezed themselves into a small space in front of the theater. There was no way to escape. El Chupacabra's growls were louder than ever.

Chapter 16

Just then, something came between them and the monster.

The Mystery Machine!

Not a moment too soon, the van puttered through the street, cutting off the monster's view of the five humans.

After the van went by, the spot in front of the theater was empty.

"Whew!" said Fred, clinging to the side of the Mystery Machine as it hurtled around a corner.

"Rooarr!" howled El Chupacabra, his growls fading into the distance.

Somehow, Daphne, Velma, Fred, Luis, and Alejo managed to climb into the van. "Jinkies!" Velma said to Shaggy. "Perfect timing! If you and Scooby hadn't showed up when you did, we'd be Mexican history."

Daphne was gripping a door handle. "Yeah, but now that we're safe from that creepy Bigfoot, you might want to slow down a little."

"I'd *love* to slow down," Shaggy answered, "but I have some bad news for you."

"What's that?" Fred asked.

"Like, I can't!" yelled Shaggy. "The brakes took a break! They don't work!"

"Yikes!" yelled everybody in the van.

"Rikes!" yelled Scooby.

"But I have some *good* news, too," Shaggy told them, suddenly sounding a lot calmer.

"Yes?" asked Alejo.

"We're out of gas." Shaggy turned the wheel to the right and the Mystery Machine sputtered to a stop.

"Wow!" said Daphne, looking out the window. "Right in front of a gas station. What are the chances of *that*?"

Luis rubbed the charm hanging around his neck. "Must be the good luck from Charlene's medallion."

Fred jumped out to fill up the van with gas. He asked the attendant to fix the brakes, too. Everybody else got out to stretch. Alejo went into the gas station and came out with a bag of ice. "Here, Luis," he said to his brother. "I got you some ice for that blow to your head. It must be pretty swollen by now."

"What happened?" asked Daphne.

Alejo answered. "I am afraid my brother was attacked by El Chupacabra and received quite a hit on the head. It knocked him . . . how do you say? . . . out cold."

Daphne clucked her tongue. "Here, let me help," she said, taking the ice from Alejo. She examined Luis's head. "Where's the bump?" she asked him. "I don't see anything."

Luis took the ice from Daphne and held it to his head. "Uh, right here," he said. "I can manage. Thank you, Daphne."

There was something strange about the way he was acting. Velma and Daphne exchanged a look.

Just then, Fred finished filling the tank, and they all climbed back into the Mystery Machine and took off. "Where to now, guys?" Fred asked from the driver's seat. "The *curandero* said to look to the past, but what exactly does that mean?"

"Look!" Velma said, pointing to a sign they were passing at that very moment. She read out loud. "Discover the Mysteries of Mexico's Past!"

Fred chimed in, reading the rest of the sign. "Visit the Museum of Anthropology!"

Velma was excited. "What better place than a museum to learn about the past?" she asked.

"Perfect," agreed Fred. "And we should be able to get there by morning." He stepped on the gas and the van speeded up.

As soon as the Mystery Machine zoomed by, a black-gloved hand reached up and took the sign away.

Chapter 17

Shaggy stretched and yawned, shielding his eyes from the bright sun pouring in through the windows of the van. "Is it morning already?" he asked. "I could sure use some more sleep."

Luis rubbed his eyes and checked out the view of Mexico City on the horizon. "I could sure use some of Charlene's coffee," he said.

Scooby was in the middle of a huge yawn when he heard that, but his eyes lit up. "Reah! Roffee!"

"Hey guys! Look!" Daphne pointed out the window at a billboard the van was passing. It was Mister Smiley, the same guy in all the billboards they'd passed in the United States — only this time he was wearing a sombrero.

Alejo read the sign out loud. "Coming soon to Veracruz — Mister Smiley's Latin Adventure!"

"Looks just like the one we have back home," Daphne said.

"Only this one's got a Spanish accent!" added Shaggy.

Luis looked glum. "If we don't solve the Chupacabra mystery, the only tourist attraction I foresee is one big, empty, ghost town."

The gang and their friends forgot all about Mister Smiley as they entered the Museum of Anthropology a little while later. The first thing they passed was a statue of Taloc, the Rain God. "The *curandero* said to look to the past," Fred said, checking out a map of the museum, "so we might as well start at the very beginning."

"Interesting," Velma said, looking at another statue they were passing. It portrayed a beast that was a combination of a man and a jaguar. "Half-man, half-beast."

Shaggy and Scooby got a kick out of that idea, and made their own half-man, half-beast "statue," intertwining their arms and legs and baring their teeth. Then Shaggy spotted something and untangled himself. "Hey, look, guys! Scooters!" He pointed to some replicas of ancient wheeled toys, looking like small dogs on wheels.

"Leave it to Shaggy to come to a museum and immediately find the toys," Daphne said. But when Shaggy and Scooby jumped onto the dogs and started scooting along, she couldn't resist. She and the others all joined in, and they raced down the hallways of the museum.

Suddenly, they found themselves deep in the darkest, farthest reaches of the museum. They got off the scooters and wandered along dark hallways and down empty echoing stairways, passing all sorts of creepy things. "Jinkies!" said Velma, when she saw a skeleton wearing a necklace of human jawbones. "This place is creepy!" There were no other tourists around.

"Good morning!"

The gang jumped. Out of nowhere, a museum guide had appeared. She had flaming red hair piled high on her head, a big smile full of big teeth, and thick glasses. "Are we enjoying ourselves in Mexico City's National Museum?" she asked brightly.

Before anyone could answer, she smiled again. "Super! And would we like a private tour of the museum, which begins with a special live, multimedia show about the Aztecs?"

Fred opened his mouth to respond, but before he could get a word out she spoke again. "Super! Please follow the green directional arrows on the floor to the special VIP auditorium." She led them out the door and down the hall into a small dark space with a small stage area and a row of cushy seats. The only light came from two flaming torches on the wall.

Everybody took a seat and faced the stage. The museum guide reached up to a large dial on the wall and turned it from "2003" to "1325." "Let's turn back the hands of time, shall we?" she asked.

The room grew even darker as smoke and incense filled the small space. Suddenly, a dragon appeared, moving as if it were alive. Scooby barked at it. "It's okay, pal," Shaggy whispered. "Like, it's only animatronics." A jaguar appeared next, and two eagles, all lowered from the ceiling by invisible wires.

The museum guide began to narrate. "The warlike Aztecs had many barbarous rituals," she said. "For example, warriors sacrificed thousands of captives on the altars atop the pyramids, often ripping out their still-beating hearts to offer to the gods."

Men dressed as warriors entered the stage, wearing animal-head masks and armed to the teeth with huge knives, swords, javelins, and arrows. Music began to play, a frenzied, pounding beat, and the warriors began to dance.

"And now I'd like a volunteer from the audience," the museum guide said perkily. Scooby and Shaggy crawled under their seats. The museum guard turned her gaze on Daphne. "How 'bout you?" she asked.

Daphne looked over at Fred as if she wished he could save her. "Uh, Freddy?"

But before he could do a thing, the museum guide grabbed Daphne by the hand and yanked her up onto the stage. At the same time, a massive stone altar rose slowly out of the floor. Daphne lay down on it, and one of the warriors put a blanket over her. The others surrounded her, still dancing their frenzied ritualistic dance.

The music and drums pounded, louder and louder. The dancing was even more intense. Colored lights began to flash as the ritual reached its height.

Then, the entire room was plunged into darkness, and the wild drumming stopped.

When the lights came back on, the museum guide and all the warriors had vanished.

So had Daphne.

Chapter 18

"**D**aphne!" yelled Fred.

Velma gasped. "She's gone!"

A chilling voice came from the loudspeakers. "You've been warned."

Then the voice continued, changing to the museum guide's cheerful tone: "Please follow the arrows to the clearly marked exit doors to your right."

Shaggy nodded. "Excellent idea! Like, just what we had in mind: exiting! Right, Scoob?"

"Reah! Rexiting!"

Fred put out a hand to stop them. "Not so fast!"

Velma grabbed them, too. "We can't leave here until we find Daphne!"

"And her kidnappers," added Alejo.

Fred looked around. "But where could they have gone?" He started to search for clues.

"Why would someone want to kidnap Daphne?" Luis asked, as he checked under a seat.

Just then, Velma found something on the floor. "Look at this," she said, picking it up. "It looks like some kind of ripped label from the warriors' costumes." She strained to read the scraps of words on the label. "Mile," she said. "Enter." She shrugged. "I wonder what that means."

"Let me see that," Fred said, taking a torch from the wall for better light. As he lifted the flaming lamp, there was a creaking from under the stage.

"Look!" said Velma. "A trapdoor!"

"I wonder where it leads to?" Alejo asked.

Fred peered into it. "My guess is that it will take us right to Daphne and her kidnappers. It sure looks like the perfect getaway."

At that, Scooby and Shaggy started to tiptoe in the opposite direction. "Speaking of getting away," Shaggy said, just as Fred grabbed his shirt collar and yanked him back toward the trapdoor.

"No way, guys," said Fred, his other hand on Scooby's collar. "There's no turning back now."

Shaking, Shaggy and Scooby followed the others. "Oh, great," said Shaggy. "A dark spooky tunnel. I *hate* dark spooky tunnels!"

Just as he said that, his feet slipped out from under him and he found himself sliding downhill, along with all his friends. "Whhoooooooaaaahhhh!" they all cried.

It was like being on a roller coaster at midnight, swooping fast down tight curves and spiraling circles. They couldn't see a thing in the pitch-black darkness.

Wham! Suddenly, they hit the bottom of the tunnel. They landed in a big pile against a mound of foam.

When everyone had caught their breath, they began to look around. "Look, here's a door!" said Velma. She felt her way along the wall to a large metal door and pulled it open, slowly and carefully.

Suddenly, the gang was blinded by bright sunlight. They felt their way outside, squinting as their eyes got used to the light. Then, in the distance, they saw the most spectacular sight they'd ever laid eyes on.

Chapter 19

Two enormous pyramids stood in the blinding sun, bigger than anything in the surrounding jungle. A wide avenue led to a huge plaza where the massive buildings stood.

"We must be at the Pyramid of San Teotihuacán!" said Alejo.

"I've read about these," Velma said. "The pyramids were created by the Olmec Indians, who built Mesoamerica's first great civilization. Those are the Pyramids of the Sun and Moon, and that is the Avenue of the Dead, leading to them."

Shaggy stared up at the looming buildings. "Groovy," he muttered.

Fred pointed to another, smaller pyramid, built in the middle of a sunken square. "Hey, it's the Pyramid of the Feathered Serpent, the 'good' god we saw a statue of at the *curandero*'s tent."

Velma pulled out her binoculars for a closer look. Then she gasped. "Look! At the top! It's Daphne!" She handed the binoculars around so everyone could see.

Sure enough, Daphne was at the top of the smaller pyramid. Her wrists were tied together and there was a blindfold over her eyes. As the gang watched, she wrestled her way out of the rope and took the blindfold off. She looked down and saw her friends far, far below. They looked as tiny as ants.

"Don't move!" Fred yelled up to her. "We'll be right there!" He took off running, and the others followed him.

By the time Fred, Velma, Luis, and Alejo reached the top, they were gasping for breath. Behind them, Scooby and Shaggy huffed and puffed their way up the tall stone steps of the pyramid, sweat pouring off them as they crawled up the last, steepest steps and collapsed at the top. "Like, if the Aztecs were so brilliant," Shaggy gasped, "why didn't they invent an elevator?"

"Relevator!" said Scooby, panting hard.

Daphne laughed. "Boy, am I glad to see you guys," she said.

"What *happened* to you?" asked Velma.

"I'm not sure," Daphne said, rubbing her wrists where the rope had cut into them. "I was blindfolded by that fake museum guard and her warrior friend."

Fred looked around. "Let's get out of here before they come back for you," he said.

As they worked their way down the steps of the pyramid, Velma noticed a life-size stone statue of the Feathered Serpent god. "That's odd," she said. "This statue wasn't here before!" As the gang looked at it, a crack ran through the statue from top to bottom. It began to crumble, right before their eyes! Then a loud alarm went off.

"What's going on?" Daphne asked. Before anyone could move, a large metal cage rose from the ground and trapped them inside.

At that moment, a huge eagle swooped down from the sky and landed on top of the cage, letting out a loud squawk. The eagle wore a ridiculously big sombrero, along with a colorful poncho.

By that time, a crowd of tourists had gathered. The eagle began to speak. "Hello, my *amigos*," it said, in a bad Spanish accent. "I am Paco, the magical talking eagle. I protect the pyramids here at the Place of the Gods."

Alejo turned to Fred. "That's the worst Spanish accent I've ever heard," he whispered.

"I know!" Fred whispered back. "He looks like a character from a tacky theme park!"

Meanwhile, even more tourists had gathered. Paco kept talking to them. "These evil tourists," he said, waving a wing at the gang in the cage, "have destroyed a sacred idol and angered the gods."

"We have done no such thing!" Alejo said. He looked angry. "This eagle is lying to you!"

"Do not believe their lies," Paco went on calmly, in his terrible accent. "When the cage lifts, you must run them out of here before they completely ruin the ruins. If you don't, the gods will seek revenge themselves, and *ay caramba,* my *amigos,* you don't want to see *that!*" As the eagle flew away, the cage lifted. The crowd of angry tourists surged toward the gang.

"Yikes!" yelled Shaggy.

"Rikes!" shouted Scooby. They took off, with the rest of the gang behind them, running as fast as they could down the steps of the pyramid.

Chapter 20

Near the bottom, Daphne spotted an opening, like a cave in the stone. "Quick!" she said. "In here!"

Inside the pyramid, it was cool and dark and very musty. The gang looked around.

"Eww!" cried Daphne. "There's a ton of spiders down here!"

"Spiders?" Shaggy asked.

"Riders?" Scooby jumped into his friend's arms as they looked around at all the creepy crawlies on the walls and ceilings.

"Uh, no, guys," Velma corrected them. "Actually, those are scorpions."

"Like, I feel much better," Shaggy said.

Alejo was still looking around. "Don't worry about the scorpions," he said. "I'm sure the rats will take care of them." He pointed to a squirming pile in a dark corner.

"Rats?" Scooby and Shaggy yelled together.

At that, the whole gang started running again, deeper into the pyramid. "Jinkies," Velma said, as they entered a large, echoing chamber. "We must be in the ancient tombs." She looked up at a skeleton hand dangling over her.

"Yikes!" yelled Shaggy. This time, he jumped into Scooby's arms.

"Don't worry, Shaggy," Fred assured him. "Everything in here is dead."

That was all it took. Shaggy and Scooby started running, and once again the rest of the gang followed them. They emerged from inside the pyramid just as the angry mob of tourists came around a corner. The chase was on.

Huge dark clouds had filled the sky while the gang was inside the pyramid. Now the sound of booming thunder began to echo in the ancient plaza. Lightning streaked all around them. The kids took off running toward the base of the Pyramid of the Moon.

Suddenly, out of nowhere, the Feathered Serpent god appeared. But this time, it was alive! The beast's brightly colored feathers were covered with writhing serpents. It took in a huge breath and blew it out, sending Shaggy and Scooby flying through the air. They landed in the top branches of a tall tree overlooking the plaza.

Meanwhile, Daphne and Velma were blown way up into the sky. When they came down, they landed on the back of a gigantic statue of a winged beast. Suddenly, it turned its head to stare at them. "Ahhhh!" the girls screamed. The statue was alive!

Fred couldn't help them. He had been swept off his feet and tumbled over to the entrance to the Pyramid of the Jaguars, which was guarded by a mural of painted jaguars. While he looked at the mural, one of the jaguars came to life, baring its teeth and hissing at him. "Ahhhh!" yelled Fred.

Over in the plaza, Alejo and Luis were being chased by the demon Tezcatlipoca, which was breathing clouds of dark smoke. The demon snarled as it let loose two black cyclones to chase down the brothers. The funnel clouds spun through the ruins, sending people running for cover.

Then Daphne and Velma's winged beast took off, flying them through the air as fast as a jet. It swooped down low, then zoomed up high, giving them a stomach-churning roller-coaster ride. Daphne's hair whipped around her face. "Jeepers!" she said. "Talk about a bad hair day!"

Below them, Fred dusted himself off as he got up off the ground. Then the painted jaguar leaped right off the mural, straight for Fred! He dodged it, just as the other jaguars on the mural came to life, their sharp teeth gleaming. They began to stalk Fred, growling horribly. Just in time, an umbrella blew off a vendor's cart. Fred grabbed it and, using it as a sword, held off his attackers. He slashed and stabbed, dancing backward as the big bad kitties tried to attack from the front and sides.

Meanwhile, up in the tree, Shaggy and Scooby looked down at the chaos below. Suddenly, Shaggy looked at the branch he was holding onto and spotted a ripe green fruit. Mmm, avocado! He plucked it, peeled it, and took a big bite. Scooby found one, too.

When Shaggy had finished his avocado, he looked down at the pit in his hand. Then he looked way below him, at Fred battling the jaguars. Shaggy threw the pit as hard as he could, beaning one of the jaguars on the head. "Ha!" he laughed. Scooby threw his pit, too. Then Shaggy and Scooby started eating avocados as fast as they could, throwing their pits down at the huge snarling cats attacking Fred.

The cats were distracted long enough to give Fred the chance to swing himself up into a tree. From an upper branch, he swung higher and higher until he let go and soared over a huge stone wall, landing in the parking lot.

Fred was safe, but Velma and Daphne were still on the ride of their lives. Suddenly, the winged beast dove straight down to the ground, landing with a hard bump. Velma and Daphne fell off and landed in a shrub, surrounded by plumes and clouds of thick black smoke. Velma's glasses flew off. "I can't see!" she cried. Daphne groped around and found them for her. Velma put them back on. "I *still* can't see!" The black smoke was swirling around them. She and Daphne fought their way through the wind and smoke, inching their way toward the shelter of a temple.

"Aahhh!" they cried, as the carved serpents on the temple wall suddenly came to life, slithering and hissing as they slid around Velma's and Daphne's ankles. The two friends hopped around madly, trying to keep the snakes from climbing their legs.

Shaggy and Scooby heard them screaming and started throwing pits at the snakes. When Daphne looked up to see where the pits were coming from, Shaggy held out his hands and lifted her and Velma up into the tree.

"Holy guacamole!" Shaggy said, biting into one more avocado. "I could eat a million of these!"

Velma eyed his round stomach. "Looks like you already have," she said.

Meanwhile, down below, Luis and Alejo were still being chased by the demon and his black tornadoes. The inky funnel clouds spun the brothers around and around until they were so dizzy they couldn't see straight. They stumbled this way and that, feeling their way through the dark smoke.

Little did they know that a tall shadowy figure was following close behind, just about to grab Alejo.

Just in time, Fred and the Mystery Machine hurtled into the plaza, coming right between Alejo and the dark figure. A door swung open, and Luis and Alejo jumped in. Alejo stared out the window as the van began to pull away. He saw the dark figure pick itself up off the ground, where it had fallen. Then, he realized who he was seeing.

"Señor Fuente!" said Alejo. "What's he doing here?"

"Trying to attack you," Fred answered grimly, as he steered the van through a crowd of tourists, searching for the rest of the gang. *Wham!* Something hit the roof of the van. Fred leaned out the window to see what it was. "Daphne!"

She had jumped out of the avocado tree and landed on the roof of the Mystery Machine. Fred drove the van back past the tree, and Velma and Shaggy jumped down, too.

Fred was grinning now. Everybody was safe. He counted on his fingers. One, two, three, four, five — oops! Somebody was missing. He turned the van around to go by the avocado tree one more time. As he passed, he spotted Scooby's tail hanging down. It was twitching and moving, as if Scooby was after something!

Shaggy reached out of his window and yanked on the

tail. Scooby fell out of the tree and landed on the roof of the van with a big loud thud. There was something in his mouth, but Fred didn't even pause to find out what it was. With his friends still up on the roof, he stepped on the gas and steered the van toward the exit.

Chapter 21

"**W**hew!" Fred said, as he watched the pyramids grow smaller in his rearview mirror. He pulled over so he and Luis and Alejo could help the others off the roof and into the van. "Where were you, Scooby?" he asked.

Scooby dropped something at Fred's feet.

It was Paco, the talking eagle! Or, at least it was *parts* of Paco. The eagle was broken into pieces, making it even more obvious that he was a complete fake.

"I am *amigos* my Paco!" the pieces squawked. *"Ay caramba! Ay caramba! Ay caramba!"*

Velma snorted. "Magical eagle, huh? I didn't buy this animatronic imposter for one minute."

"Neither did Scooby!" Shaggy said proudly. "He would never attack a *real* bird, but he sure went after this phony."

Daphne shook her head. "I guess the *curandero* was right. Things in Mexico aren't always what they seem."

Fred stepped back toward the van. "Come on," he urged the others. "We better get out of here before these mysterious mischief makers try to top themselves."

They all piled into the van and headed back to the hotel. Back in Veracruz, the gang drove straight to the cemetery. It was time for the Day of the Dead festivities.

The gang was amazed at what they saw when they walked into the cemetery. Dusk was falling, but the area was aglow with the light of hundreds of colored candles. Children were placing bright bouquets on the gravestones, carving pumpkins, and painting a colorful fun mural full of dancing skeletons. The women of the community were bringing in platters heaped full of goodies: fruits, candies, and skeleton-shaped cookies. A vendor sold skull-shaped Popsicles, skeleton-shaped tamales, and little chocolate coffins. The gang watched with interest as a photographer took a picture of some children in brightly colored homemade masks.

Someone — or some*thing* — else was watching, too. A huge hairy paw parted the flowering underbrush near the iron fence surrounding the cemetery, and two glowing green eyes watched as Luis and Alejo and the gang walked along the paths between the gravestones.

Scooby and Shaggy were both shaking a little as they gazed around at the tombstones and the skeletons. But Scooby's shaking stopped when he spotted Chiquita at the other end of the cemetery. He picked up his head and swaggered along, showing off for her, until he walked right into a tombstone. "Rouch!" he said, rubbing his head. Chiquita giggled.

Luis and Alejo and the gang approached the bench where Doña Dolores and Sofia sat, surrounded by the other village women.

"How awful!" one of them was saying. "To witness something like that!"

"You are so strong, Dolores," another told her. "Like a bull."

A third woman whispered to the woman sitting next to her, "Some people have all the luck. Why can't El Chupacabra carry off *my* future daughter-in-law?"

"Señora!" said Doña Dolores in a shocked tone, just as Alejo and Luis arrived at the bench.

"What's going on?" Alejo asked, seeing that his mother and Sofia were upset. "Are you all right?"

"Where's Charlene?" Luis asked, looking around in bewilderment.

Doña Dolores held up her hands. "Please calm down, both of you. There is nothing to be upset about," she began. Then she took a big breath and began to shout hysterically to Luis, "EL CHUPACABRA HAS RUN OFF WITH YOUR FIANCÉE! WE'LL NEVER SEE HER AGAIN!" She began to sob.

Luis's face went white.

"Please," said Alejo, "somebody tell us what happened."

Sofia took over. "It all started just moments after you left. We were in the café. El Chupacabra broke down the door, picked up Charlene in his arms, and ran off with her!"

Luis couldn't believe his ears. "Charlene! This is terrible. I never should have left!"

"Jinkies," said Velma. She and the gang had been listening closely to the whole story. "And she's still missing?"

Sofia nodded. "Yes. We've been looking for her since yesterday. The villagers are continuing the search here at the cemetery and up in the hills."

Nearby, the children began to play monster games. "Grrrowl!" said Jorge, holding up his hands as he stalked toward a little girl. "I am El Chupacabra! I am going to eat you!"

"All this talk of El Chupacabra is not good for the children," Sofia said. She turned to Jorge and his friends. "Now forget about all this scary monster stuff," she told them, "and play with your skeletons among the tombstones!"

It sounded so funny that Daphne and Velma almost giggled.

Luis pulled himself up straighter. "I must go join the search," he said.

"Yes," said Fred, taking out a small notebook. "But it'll be more productive if we get all our facts straight first."

Chapter 22

Fred began to write, taking notes as he spoke. "I think the village is being terrorized for a reason," he said thoughtfully. "Somebody wants to scare everyone off and get us out of the way."

"But what's to be gained by *that*?" Daphne asked.

Velma thought she knew. "El Chupacabra is scaring off the tourists, making businesses suffer."

Fred nodded. "If the Oteros are forced to sell, Señor Fuente gets what he wants. The Oteros' land."

Daphne was beginning to understand. "Good point," she said. "But what does that have to do with El Chupacabra?"

Fred thought some more. "The footprints leading away from the cottage suggested El Chupacabra was scared off once Shaggy alerted the rest of us."

"Yeah," put in Shaggy. "Like, he was okay scaring Scooby and me, but chickened out at the thought of facing more people. Some monster."

Velma's eyes lit up. "Maybe he's a fake!"

But Daphne wasn't so sure. "I don't think we can rule out the supernatural."

Alejo and Luis spoke up together. "Supernatural?"

"If the creatures at the pyramids were special effects," Daphne explained, "they were pretty *special*."

Shaggy agreed. "And very *effective*."

"Real or fake," Velma said, "someone's been following us."

Fred looked over his shoulder. "Yeah, they're anticipating our every move. But how?"

Velma pulled out her camcorder. "Let's look at my videotape again," she suggested. She hit the "Play" button. On the monitor, Fred was walking down the street, just about to discover the painted warning on the van.

"Freeze the frame!" Fred said. Velma hit the "Pause" button. "Look." Fred pointed at the screen. "Whoever wrote *mañana,* the Spanish word for 'tomorrow,' forgot the tilde."

"What's a tilde?" Shaggy asked.

Fred wrote the symbol in his notebook and showed it to everybody. "It's a symbol you put over the *n* to change the pronunciation. Without it, the word would be said incorrectly as 'manana,' instead of 'man-ya-na,' a mistake no *real* Spanish-speaking person would make."

Velma looked at Fred admiringly. "Looks like your Spanish lessons are finally paying off," she said.

"Sí!" Alejo agreed.

Shaggy was still figuring it out. "So, the bad guy doesn't speak Spanish?"

"Maybe," Fred answered. "But there's always the possibility that there's more than *one* bad guy."

Daphne thought of something. "Velma," she asked, "did you save the torn label from the fake warrior's costume?"

Velma felt around in her pockets, then held the label out to Daphne. "Sure did," she said. "But I still don't know what it means."

Just then, Doña Dolores and Sofia walked up to the gang. "Sorry to interrupt," Doña Dolores said, "but it's time for us to pay our respects. We're all ready to go."

"Please feel free to join us," Sofia urged the gang.

It was totally dark out by then. Carrying candles, they all walked over to Señor Otero's grave, beneath a beautiful flowering bush. Lovingly, Sofia lay a woolen sweater down on the grave. Alejo arranged a handful of jalapeño peppers near it. Doña Dolores propped a photograph of the whole family against the tombstone. Luis added a bowl of salsa. "My homemade mango salsa," he said sadly. "His favorite." He stepped forward again and put down a cup. "And from Charlene, a cup of her *cafe lechera*." He let out a long sigh. "Maybe if he knows where she is, he will send us a sign."

He stepped back to join the others, just as a wisp of smoke rose from the grave and transformed into the shape of a ghost. A ghost with the face of a distinguished older man with a bushy mustache.

Then the apparition spoke. "I am the ghost of Señor Otero."

Chapter 23

Doña Dolores looked terrified. Her face turned white and she gasped.

"Don't be alarmed," said the ghost. "As you all know, today is the day we spirits return to Earth to commune with the living. Normally we aren't seen or heard, but I have an especially important message to bring to you."

At that, Doña Dolores fainted. Alejo and Luis caught her and sat her down on a bench while Sofia gave her a gentle slap on the cheek to wake her up. "Mama," Alejo pleaded. "Please, wake up!"

Doña Dolores opened her eyes.

The ghost continued to speak. "I have learned that El Chupacabra is the result of an evil curse placed on our land," he told his family. "The only way to break the spell is to get rid of that land. I beg my family to sell everything at once."

Shocked, the gang exchanged glances. Fred leaned over and whispered something to Daphne. Daphne passed it on to Velma. Velma nodded.

"Once the land is sold," the ghost went on, "El Chupacabra will vanish forever and Charlene will be returned, unharmed."

After that, he seemed to be finished with his speech. But he still hovered in front of them, over his tombstone.

Luis clutched the medallion Charlene had given him. "Charlene," he whispered to himself. He turned the medallion over and over in his hand. Fred, looking over from his seat next to Luis, noticed a small button on the back side of it.

Alejo stood up to speak. "That doesn't look or sound *anything* like my father!" he said, pointing to the ghost. "Someone is playing tricks on us!"

Fred leaned over to Luis. "Can I see your medallion?" he asked. Luis handed it to him.

"Just as I suspected," said Fred, after he'd examined it for a moment. "It's a tracking device. Let's see if it works in reverse." He pressed the button.

Nothing happened.

Except that Scooby's ears pricked up. He held his head to one side, listening to something only he could hear. Only he — and Chiquita and the other dogs in the cemetery. Scooby began to walk away, following the high-pitched sound. Like a sleepwalker, he marched over to a large stone building in the middle of the cemetery, a mausoleum where a whole family was buried. Scooby pushed open the massive stone door.

Inside, a man in a skeleton costume jiggled a joystick, controlling a complicated machine full of lights and buttons. In the middle of the control panel was a monitor showing the cemetery. The monitor also showed the ghost of Señor Otero — obviously nothing but a laser show!

Scooby pointed at the man and began to bark. The other dogs joined in.

"Stop that now!" the man in the costume yelled. "Be quiet! Do you hear me? Quiet!"

The dogs only barked louder. People in the cemetery started to look.

The man tried to kick the door shut, still holding onto his controls. He couldn't budge the door, especially with Chiquita snapping at his feet.

The rest of the gang showed up just then. They watched as the man fiddled desperately with his buttons and spoke into the microphone. "Please!" he said, forgetting to use the ghost voice. "Ignore the stupid dog! Pay no attention to the man behind the curtain! Leave the cemetery at once! It is cursed! The whole town is cursed! Sell the land and everything will return to normal!"

Fred just laughed as he watched the man try to keep the ghost illusion alive. "Can't you see?" Fred asked. "Many of the people here don't understand you. Speaking Spanish might help!"

The man in the skeleton costume turned to him. "I don't know *how* to speak Spanish!" he yelled. "Why can't everyone just learn English?" With that, he threw down his joystick and made a break for it, dashing out the door.

The gang blocked him. "Like, not so fast," Shaggy said. He reached out and pulled the skeleton mask right off the man's face.

Chapter 24

"**I**t's Mister Smiley!" yelled Fred.

The man from the billboards stared back at them. He looked exactly like his picture — except that he was definitely *not* smiling now.

Daphne gestured to some policemen who had appeared nearby. "Officers, if you will," she said. They came forward and snapped a pair of handcuffs onto Mister Smiley's wrists.

By then, all the Oteros and a crowd of other interested people had gathered near the mausoleum. Velma took the label out of her pocket again and held it up. "We suspected that 'mile' and 'enter' were part of bigger words, and look, we were right!" She walked over to the mausoleum and pulled out a briefcase she had spotted. It had the Smiley Entertainment logo plastered across it. "See?" Velma asked. "Smiley Entertainment." She held up the label to show how it fit across part of the logo. "When Mister Smiley was unable to convince the locals to sell their land for his new theme park, he turned to the Otero family."

Fred joined her in the explanation. "Their hotel is built

on some of the best real estate in Veracruz. When they refused to sell, he wouldn't take no for an answer."

Daphne chimed in. "So he terrorized the tourists with the Chupacabra attacks, hoping to ruin the Oteros' hotel business and force them to sell."

"And then he did everything he could," added Velma, "to prevent us from revealing his scheme."

"Smiley was the perfect person to pull it off," Fred finished.

Luis was looking from one person to the other as he listened. But he still looked confused. "But why?" he asked simply.

"Please," Mister Smiley said, pretending to be bored with the long explanation. "You're only encouraging him."

Fred ignored their prisoner. "Being the head of a theme park, he had access to the best special effects money can buy, whether it was realistic costumes, like those jaguars that were chasing me, or the holograms of the serpents that 'came alive,' or the laser image of the ghost of Señor Otero."

Shaggy nodded. "Like, not to mention the animatronic animals like our 'magical' eagle friend, Paco."

Daphne went on with the story. "And by kidnapping me and framing us as vandals, he was able to derail our investigation *and* provide bad publicity for the pyramids —"

"Soon to be his chief competitor for the dollars of tourists in Mexico from all over the world," finished Velma.

Shaggy stroked his chin, looking wise. "Our deductions make perfect sense," he said. "But if Smiley is behind the

Chupacabra attacks, then how do we explain — *that*?!" He pointed to the bell tower of the church that overlooked the graveyard. It was lit up so that it stood out in the darkness, white and tall. At the very top were two blazing green lights.

The eyes of El Chupacabra!

Chapter 25

The monster threw back his head, opened his mouth wide to show off his sharp white teeth, and moaned a long, drawn-out howl that made everyone shiver.

"That sure doesn't look like a special effect to me!" said Daphne, hugging herself.

Sofia looked terrified. "It is the monster!"

"El Chupacabra!" shouted Luis. "*¡Vámanos!* Let's go!"

Shaggy exchanged a frightened look with Scooby. They both gulped. "Like, this is going to be bad," Shaggy said. "Real bad."

Above them, El Chupacabra grabbed onto the rope of the church bell. He swung back and forth, higher and higher, his growls growing louder and louder. Finally, he let go and flew through the air, landing on the roof of the church. He was much closer now, and the crowd drew back in fear. Some parents grabbed their children and headed for the main gate. Others chose to stand their ground. They weren't ready to give up their town to the monster.

Up on the church roof, El Chupacabra reached up and tore the brick chimney right off. He began to hurl the bricks at the people below. One of the bricks whizzed right by Shaggy's left ear. "Zoinks!" he said. "That could've hurt!"

Then El Chupacabra leaped off the roof and landed with a thud on the ground. He spotted a table loaded with food — and flipped the whole thing over.

Fred grabbed the table and held it up like a shield. "You don't scare us," he shouted, "you Bigfoot wanna-be!"

El Chupacabra ignored Fred, picking up pots, pans, and dishes and throwing them at the villagers. Fred held up the table to protect the crowd, and the pots bounced off it.

El Chupacabra roared in frustration. He lurched toward a stone drinking fountain and hurled it in the air, followed by a wooden bench, a family's entire picnic, and all the instruments in the band.

The monster was on the rampage. He had to be stopped!

Velma snuck up behind El Chupacabra, picked up a guitar he'd just tossed, and bashed it over his head. That stopped him for a moment! He rubbed his head and staggered, stumbling into the demolished drum set with a *crash* and a *bang*.

When he regained his balance, he looked around as if trying to figure out what horrible thing he could do next. With the loudest growl ever, he took off after a group of children who were trying to get a better look at him. The children screamed and scattered. Luis and Alejo and several other parents tried to get between them and the monster. In the chaos, Luis's medallion flew off his neck. Fred caught it as he ran by.

Daphne picked up a glowing jack-o'-lantern and heaved it at the monster. He dodged it, his growling silenced for a moment. Was the monster afraid of fire?

Velma grabbed another jack-o'-lantern and threw it at El Chupacabra. It missed — and landed right on Shaggy's head!

Velma tried again. This time, she aimed at the monster's legs, throwing the pumpkin like a bowling ball. The pumpkin knocked El Chupacabra right off his feet! He fell over backward. While he was struggling to his feet, Shaggy let loose a whole bunch of dogs that had been tied to a fence. Scooby and Chiquita joined the pack as they ran after the monster, barking madly.

El Chupacabra ran in circles, the dogs at his heels. In the crowd, somebody began to giggle. For a huge scary monster, he looked pretty silly. Soon the whole crowd was laughing as the dogs backed El Chupacabra up against a fence in the corner of the cemetery. He growled as loudly as he could, but the dogs' barking drowned him out. Finally, desperately, El Chupacabra lunged for Chiquita and picked her up. The little Chihuahua looked tinier than ever in his huge hairy hands.

Jorge screamed.

Scooby flew into action, taking a running start to jump right at the monster's head. Meanwhile, up above, Daphne and Velma had climbed to the roof of the church. They were cutting the strings that held up some colorful lanterns and piñatas. They raised their arms, holding their makeshift net over the monster as Scooby came toward him.

Then Scooby leaped! Unfortunately, his aim wasn't great. He landed with his arms around El Chupacabra's head, his tummy against the monster's hairy face.

Blinded, the monster dropped Chiquita. She scampered toward Jorge and safety. At the same time, Daphne and Velma dropped their net. The wires and ropes fell over the monster. He roared loudly as he struggled and twisted around, getting more and more tangled in the wires and ropes and lanterns and piñatas. He fell over with a thud, and one of the piñatas broke open and spilled candies and toys all over his head.

Scooby, much smaller than the monster, managed to squirm his way out of the net and get away.

El Chupacabra rolled over and over, trying to get free. He reached out to the branch of a tree, grabbing at it to help himself up. A beehive fell off the tree and split into pieces, sending angry bees swarming all over the monster. He roared and ran in circles, but the bees wouldn't let him be. He raced around and around, tripping over tombstones and dodging parents and children and dogs, waving his huge hairy hands wildly as he tried to keep the bees off his face.

Scooby motioned to Chiquita. Each of them picked up an end of a fallen piece of wire. The two dogs held the wire in their teeth, holding it in the monster's way so that when he came running toward them at full speed, he tripped and tumbled over and over, somersaulting right into the big fountain in the center of the cemetery.

Two policemen appeared and slapped a gigantic pair of handcuffs onto the beast while the villagers applauded and cheered.

"They caught the monster!" yelled Jorge happily.

"Well," said Fred, "we caught *something,* but 'monster' might be a little strong." He reached out to grab El Chupacabra. With a quick motion, he unzipped the monster's furry chest!

Chapter 26

As the monster costume fell away, out stepped a familiar figure. Big red hair, thick glasses, a huge smile with huge teeth — it was the museum guide!

She threw aside the stilts she had been using inside the costume and smiled her big smile. "Well," she said sheepishly, "we certainly weren't expecting *that,* were we?"

The policemen stepped forward and, using a smaller pair of handcuffs, made sure that she couldn't get away.

Mister Smiley spoke up. "Please, leave her alone!" he pleaded. "She only did what I asked her to do. I'm the guilty one, not her."

Daphne shook her head. "Hardly," she said. "It takes two to tango."

"I'm afraid she's right," said the museum guide. "Smiley didn't have to pull my leg to be part of his scheme. I love him! You see, I worked as an actress and stuntwoman at his theme park."

Suddenly, Mister Smiley wore a goofy look. "When I visited one day, it was love at first sight," he murmured, gazing at the red-haired woman.

"Speaking of love," Luis said, "where is my fiancée, Charlene?"

The museum guide blushed and stammered. "I — I'm afraid you won't be seeing her ever again," she said. Then she went on in her usual cheerful tone. "I suggest you pick up the pieces of your shattered life and find someone new."

Luis stared at her in disbelief. "What? What are you saying?"

Mister Smiley nodded sadly. "Uh, just like the lady said," he told Luis. "You won't ever see her again."

Luis began to sob. "I can't accept that," he said. Looking up at the sky, he pleaded, "Papa, I asked for a sign, *anything,* to show us where Charlene might be. Please! Don't let your firstborn son down!" He walked slowly over to his father's grave and looked at the gifts the family had placed there.

The others followed him. Sofia gasped. "Look!" she said. "The gifts we left for him are gone!"

"Not all of them," Fred noticed.

Alejo took a closer look at the almost-empty grave. "The only thing that's left is the *cafe lechera* that Charlene made for him," he said wonderingly.

Just then, a huge gust of wind picked up the cup and lifted it right into the air. It fell to the ground and shattered into pieces, right at the feet of the museum guide.

Luis looked bewildered. "I don't understand," he said.

"I'm beginning to," Velma said.

"I was afraid of that," said the museum guide.

At that moment, Scooby trotted over and started to lick the guide's feet. She giggled and tried to move away. But Scooby kept licking. Shaggy looked down to see what

Scooby was tasting. "Look!" he said, pointing. "Scooby's licking coffee grounds from her feet!"

Daphne opened her bag and pulled out the plaster cast she had made of El Chupacabra's huge footprint. "Which look exactly like the gritty substance I found in this footprint at the cottages," she said.

Velma frowned. "Hmm," she said. "I seem to recall someone mentioning coffee grinds" — she put on a broad Texas accent — "'comin' out of their ears' from working in the café all day." With that, she walked over to the museum guide and snatched off her red hair, revealing blond hair underneath. Then she snatched off the woman's glasses — and her fake teeth.

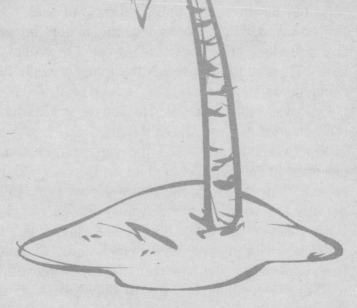

Chapter 27

"**C**harlene!" shouted Luis.

"Like, Scooby sure is good at picking out the phonies," Shaggy said admiringly, "whether they're eagles or redheads!"

Scooby blushed at the praise. "Raww," he said.

Fred was nodding. "So it was *Smiley* in the Chupacabra costume who carried you out of the café," he said to Charlene. "Then you took over as the monster while he became the warrior."

Luis was still in shock. He stared at Charlene. "I thought you loved me," he said sadly.

"Oh, wake up and smell the caffay lay-chair-a, you pea-brained romantic," Charlene said, in her old Texas accent. "I never loved you! I loved your money! If we got married, your inheritance would become mine! Then I was fixin' to drop you like a hot tamale and share my riches with my little honeybunch here." She did her best, considering the handcuffs, to link arms with Mister Smiley, cuddling up next to him with a charming smile.

Mister Smiley faced Luis. "But that goody-goody brother of yours had to complicate everything." He glared at Alejo. "Mister 'I-want-to-respect-father's-wishes' over there."

Just then, Señor Fuente ran up, panting. "Oh, thank goodness you're all okay!" he said.

"Señor Fuente!" said Alejo. "What are you doing here?"

Señor Fuente ignored the question. "Thank goodness you're all okay," he repeated.

Luis stared at him. "You mean, you knew about all of this?"

"Please," begged Señor Fuente, "let me explain. I admit I tried to convince you to sell your land. But I finally accepted that you would never go against your father's wishes, and I respected that. Just as Luis came to accept and respect it." He turned to Mister Smiley and Charlene, who were still snuggled up as close as they could be. "But these two characters don't understand things like loyalty and family. When I heard of their harebrained Bigfoot scheme, I tried to track you down at the pyramids — not to harm you, but to warn you!"

Alejo stepped forward to shake the man's hand. "I understand," he said. "Please accept my apologies."

Señor Fuente took his hand. Then he hugged Alejo.

Then Fred handed Luis his medallion. "And please accept *our* apologies, Luis," he said. "I have to admit, there were times when we questioned your integrity. We were wrong."

Luis nodded toward Charlene and Mister Smiley. "Well, with con artists like *these* two in the world," he held up the medallion, "tracking our every move —"

"Removing brake fluid from your car, putting up fake road signs —" continued Alejo.

"I can see now how 'misunderstandings' happen," Luis finished. "From now on, I will try to look beyond the surface to what lies beneath."

Charlene turned to Mister Smiley. "What happens now, hon?" she asked.

"We go to *jail*," answered Smiley. "Whattaya *think* happens? We could've made *billions*, if it hadn't been for those meddling kids!"

The cops led the two con artists away. Doña Dolores watched them go. "I never trusted Señorita Charlene, that *bruja*," she muttered.

Shaggy heard her. *"Bruja?"*

"Witch," Fred translated.

Everybody cracked up.

Daphne looked around at the mess the "monster" had made of the cemetery. "Let's get this place back in shape," she suggested.

"Yeah," said Velma. "We have a celebration to . . . celebrate!"

The gang headed off to salvage the Day of the Dead festivities, leaving Luis and Alejo on their own near their father's grave. "Alejo," said Luis, "I have something to confess."

"Yes, brother?"

"When you called out for help, I *did* hear you. But I was paralyzed with fear. After losing Papa last year, I panicked at the thought of losing my only brother. So I lied and said Bigfoot knocked me out. I'm sorry for being a coward. I pray it never happens again."

Alejo put an arm around his brother's shoulders. "Hey,

there are worse things than being a coward," he said, as they headed over to join the others.

Just then, Shaggy walked by and heard what Alejo had said. "Yeah," he agreed happily. "I've made a career out of it!"

Chapter 28

Within an hour, the cemetery had been restored to order. The lanterns were glowing and the food had been cleaned up and set out on the tables. The musicians had picked up their instruments and dusted them off, and they were playing sweet music that filled the night air.

The Scooby gang and the Otero family sat on picnic blankets, eating all the delicious food they had brought.

"So," Daphne said, "I guess there never was a real Chupacabra. I wonder how *that* myth got started."

"Like all myths, I guess," Velma said thoughtfully. "Since the beginning of time, men and women have loved to tell stories. And what better reason for creating them than to explain the many things we can never understand and maybe never will?"

Shaggy got to his feet, holding up a dripping sweet mango. "Yeah," he agreed, "like, how they can pack so much flavor into one piece of fruit!"

Everybody laughed.

Then Doña Dolores stood up and brushed herself off. "Well," she said, "at least our ancestors had the good sense to create a way to work off all those calories." She held out a hand to Shaggy. Leading him out to an open grassy area, she began to shake her hips to the beat, leading him into a conga line that the others jumped up to join. Soon all the gang and all the Otero relatives were dancing, with Scooby at the end of the line. Happily, Scooby shook a pair of maracas as he followed Chiquita, moving to the beat. "R-r-r-r-adios!" he called.

ON A QUEST
FOR FUN WITH

Fight 'em

Pose 'em

Display 'em

ALL NEW SAMURAI JACK™
TOYS AVAILABLE AT
A RETAILER NEAR YOU.

 Equity Marketing, Inc.

Equity Marketing Inc.,
Los Angeles CA 90048